The Twelve Groans of Christmas

Jeremy Moorhouse

DEDICATION

For all those people, who like me, find the whole ghastly
business a bit of a chore.
Bah-Humbug!

CONTENTS

ACKNOWLEDGMENTS

I'd like to thank Royal Mail, for the 17 Christmases I worked in that environment, and the entire corporate world, for curing me of Christmas, and for providing so much to write about the whole ludicrous business.

1. BLACKMAIL!

The board of directors all congratulated one another as they looked over the figures and drooled over the next round of bonus payments. By hell they'd done well. They'd managed to persuade the fools to give even more than they had last year.

Never mind Santa on his sleigh, Fat Bob in marketing was going to be getting far more than a few pressies under the tree. He was going to be able to spend weeks at 'The red lights of Bulgaria' massage and pleasure salon. There ought to be enough left over to pay the wife's tennis club outing bill too.

Linda in distribution was thrilled, she'd spent so much on fuel for the fleet that not only would she be getting a directors bonus, she had about a million Texaco star points too. Linda had her heart set on the new 4-foot, authentic rock and pond weed finish solar illuminated patio pond, now she could get two!

Gerald in sales had been congratulating himself for months already. You had to have an ego like Gerald's if you wanted to get on. "It doesn't matter who they are, just keep on talking over them." was his motto.

Their message had been simple, join in or we'll make you look like a right miserable sod!

They'd done their market research too.

"But I just want to spend the day on my own." A few people had said.

"Challenge accepted "Rita from analysis had said. "We can either portray them as victims, or as miserable gits" and then "and never mind they spend about 51 weeks of the year being ignored, we need to make them feel guilty, so they spend some and join in."

It had worked of course, just like all those Christmas films had taught everyone. Take for instance Charles Dickens with Scrooge bless him.

The message was clear, if you don't join in, you're abnormal! You're either a miserable sod, or you're so horrible no one else wants to see you!

Quite plainly, it was Blackmail.

The twelve Groans of Christmas

2. PLASTIC.

Julie loved Christmas; she loved seeing all the houses covered in lights. This year she was going for the Christmas cup which was a trophy she and her neighbours competed for every December. The winner got a bottle of Aldi Bucks fizz too. Everyone put five pounds in a pot and the homeowners put out collection boxes for the visitors to express their appreciation. The collection was then donated to a business, (oops sorry) , charity of their choice.

Julie had persuaded her neighbours Geoff and Mary to team up and in just a few minutes, they would be round to begin the unboxing of all the new lights and inflatable snowmen they'd bought.

It took a long time and three ladders to get the flashing

icicles up. They put the empty boxes in a pile. They had a big Santa on a sleigh in the middle of the two houses and an illuminated 'Seasons Greetings' sign to hang over it.

This was framed by six plastic Christmas trees complete with flashing balls.

Eventually, the walls were covered, and it was time to unwrap the plastic Twinkle Reindeers and the four Jolly Elves. By the time they'd unwrapped the inflatable snowman, they had a grand total of twenty-two plugs to connect to a power supply.

Geoff and Mary agreed to run everything on the lawns from their garage, and Julie would power the Icicles and sleigh and flashing plastic Christmas trees from her back passageway. Mary set off to the DIY store to get some additional multiple input adapters.

There were still more plastic delights to unwrap. Geoff had bought a festive plastic Igloo with a happy Eskimo fishing. When it was lit up, the Eskimo's fishing rod would go up and down and a voice wishing everyone a Happy Christmas would come from a tiny speaker fitted cleverly in his bottom.

And there was still more. There were brightly coloured illuminated candy canes, and Julies favourite, a trio of angels.

The pile of packaging alone was almost big enough to fill

Geoff and Mary's driveway. Heaven knows how much electric they would use while they did their bit to light the street.

There was so much plastic in fact, that the Chinese ambassador for exports would have been proud of them.

At last it was all ready and there was only one thing left to do. The trio set about breaking down all the cardboard packaging and packing up all the plastic bags and ties and other nameless strands of cellophane and PVC.

They made sure everything was packed up and ready for the recycling men. They always did their recycling. Of course more than half the plastics would end up dumped on land fill in Madagascar of Malaysia, but at least they were doing their bit for the environment!

3. PICKLES

Terry was grumpy, but this was a task he'd been given, and it was one of the very few contributions he made for the annual re-run of Saturnalia.

Bloody Romans!

He liked the food. He liked being able to go to Halfords with his vouchers and buy gadgets he'd never use. He especially liked all the extra opportunities to pour beer down his throat. What he loathed was having to go shopping.

Marjorie had given him a list and if he couldn't get what she wanted in Bodmin, he would have to drive to Liskeard, or maybe even Saltash. The prospect was horrible. It was the 20th of December and Terry had thought he'd beat the queues by going early on a Sunday. He'd arrived at Asda forty-five minutes before

opening time, only to discover there was already a
considerable queue of eager shoppers, all equipped
with the new monster trollies.

Monster trollies had an extra basket located on rods
above the main section. It gave people somewhere safe
to pile up the pringles and selection boxes. Monster
trollies for monster people Terry had thought as he
reluctantly took one himself and went to join the
queue.

He had to grudgingly admit, he was impressed. Some of
this lot really knew what they were doing. Some of
them had brought breakfast with them and were busy
shovelling pop tarts and sausages rolls down in between
drags of skinny roll ups. There were murmurings about
Brussel sprouts and Advocaat.

At last the doors opened and the excited customers
squeezed through the doors and headed for their
favourite sections of the shop.
Most of them went to the aisles with the highest sugar
content.

Terry winced; George Michael was on the speakers
bemoaning his fate again. Terry wondered if George
had ever had a good Christmas and why the hell he
couldn't have written a song about that instead of this
bloody dreary dirge.

Terry headed for the back of the checkouts and then
turned sharply into the aisle as he saw the sign that

corresponded to his list.

Gherkins

Pickled Onions

Red cabbage

Beetroot, sliced (but get whole if they've run out)

2 jars of Branston pickle

Piccalilli

Capers

There was a section of empty shelves with a message from the manager saying the company regretted that demand had outstripped availability. The only available item was capers, there were hundreds of little jars. Who on earth eats capers? Terry thought to himself. "Bugger!"

He stomped toward the checkout where he ungraciously thunked the jar of capers on the conveyor. A young woman in a tabard approached him from behind. "Would you like to use our self-checkout sir?"

"Why? What's wrong with this one?" He answered in an unusually surly tone. "Every time someone uses one of those it helps put another one of your colleagues out of a job!"

The poor girl was just trying to do her job, and she didn't really need Terry to tell her what she already knew. "Have a lovely Christmas" she smiled and retained her professional composure with a grace which Terry clearly lacked.

He went to Morrisons next. There was a queue to get in the car park cause by an old lady who was trying to get a 12-foot Norwegian pine into her Smart Car.
It was 11.55 when Terry finally got to the pickles section. The hordes of Bodmin had clearly arrived before him and the shelves were a sorry picture of empty cardboard trays and a few jars of pickling vinegar. There were a few jars of red cabbage though, so he took two, just in case there was nothing else anywhere. As he made his way grumpily to the checkout his phone beeped. "Can you get some mayonnaise too please" the message said. He doubled back. The only mayonnaise was the potion which declared itself 'reduced calorie'. Terry had been caught out with that one before and decided he'd rather smother his salad in white emulsion. Perhaps Sainsburys would have some. He managed to reach the checkout before George began singing his tale of woe again.

At Sainsbury's there was a skinny man in a red and white outfit at the door greeting shoppers and ringing a bell loudly. "Oh god" Terry groaned. He made his way into the shop avoiding making eye contact with Santa. Feeling optimistic, he took a basket. The fairy tale of New York was playing. "Oh great!" he muttered sarcastically "and now the bloody Christmas wife beating song". Terry hated that one with a passion. Just past the sprout section was a big display of mayonnaise and Branston pickle. It was all in 3 litre containers though, and he didn't really need that much. He had to go back when he discovered that all that was left on the pickles section was Red cabbage and the inevitable capers. There were some pickled eggs though. They weren't on the list, but he picked up a jar anyway.

Surely there were some pickled onions somewhere? He thought he'd escaped but once again, the sound of George reached his ears. "For fucks sake" he growled to himself between clenched teeth.

On his way out he stopped to watch an argument between two families who were fighting over the last Swede and Brussel Sprout bargain twin pack.
Funny really, neither family looked as if vegetables were usually very high on their list of priorities.

He paused in the car park. Where now? Perhaps the Co-op in town would have beetroot and piccalilli?

Parking cost Terry 70 pence and he wasn't happy about it. He'd have to walk nearly 300 yards too. He huffed and puffed along the street and his spirits were momentarily lifted as he realised the co-op was relatively quiet. He braced himself and stepped inside. Apparently snow was falling all around Shakin Stevens. Terry wondered where he was. In Bodmin it wasn't even chilly, and the day was another normal wet, damp, mizzly, moorland day.

Terry was inordinately pleased to discover that the Co-op had beetroot. Then he saw the price. The empty shelves he'd viewed in the other three shops had all advertised beetroot for less than 50p a jar. It was £1.80 in the Co-Op. Shakey finished and George got going again. There was more swearing, and Terry stomped to the till with the jar.

All that was left to get was piccalilli. Terry went to the spar shop. The lad on the counter said they didn't sell piccalilli. He exited just as the first few bars of Last Christmas began to play from some unknown but inescapable source.

Next he went to the Londis shop by the school. George was waffling away in there too. The woman behind the counter looked at him as if he'd asked to buy Rocking horse manure.

He was sitting in his car feeling dejected when, like a light through the clouds on a stormy day, he remembered that B&M sold food. If he was quick, he'd make it.

He couldn't believe the queue just for the car park. Although it was late on a Sunday afternoon now, for shopping that was, it looked as if half the town had suddenly remembered they needed some more plastic substandard vacuous tat, and they had massed at the very place Terry wanted to visit now.

He was getting even more tense, which really wasn't necessary. Then again, lots of people liked to have their biggest dramas at Christmas time. He flicked on the radio but rapidly flicked it off again when the advert to go and see the festive elves at Greenacres Garden Centre came on. If Terry met an Elf at this particular moment, unless it was giving away jars of piccalilli, he'd probably punch it's little festive lights out.

He didn't bother locking his car and practically sprinted for the automatic doors. The aisle was thick with people, but Terry boldly forged his way to the pickle section where behold, there was everything which had been on his list in abundance.

All that ruddy time and he could have just come here in the first place.

George began to play on the stores hidden speakers.

Terry raised his eyes to the ceiling where he imagined the noise was emanating and with complete disregard for his whereabouts shouted loudly "I don't care about your last fucking Christmas! Just shut up and leave me the fuck alone!" The crowd in the aisle parted like the Red Sea. Terry snatched a jar of pickle and ignoring all the shocked looks made his way to the checkout.

He'd just returned to the car when his phone rang. It was a short conversation.

"Yes I got everything.

Yes I got the mayonnaise.

Yes, everything.

Yes even piccalilli."

As he drove home and reflected on his day, he couldn't help but feel dismayed. By Boxing day, everyone in his household would have eaten so much rich food they'd all be reaching for their assorted heartburn remedies.

The last thing anyone would want would be something which had been soaked in vinegar.

Most of this stuff probably wouldn't get touched until summer.

Except the piccalilli. No one in Terry's house even like piccalilli.

4. THE CHRISTMAS TREE

"I want a real tree, not a bloody plastic imitation."
Nicola was angry now, the discussion, or rather power
struggle, had been raging for twenty minutes.

Jay didn't want a real tree. Even if they got one with
roots, their little flat on the seafront didn't have a
garden to put it in afterwards, and he didn't have any
gardening tools to plant it in a wood somewhere.
Inevitably it would be him that cleaned up the needles
as Nicola had a vacuum cleaner phobia, and then there
was the problem of dealing with the dead stalk.

"Well I'm going to the farm shop, so I'll pick one without
you then!" She told him in her best exasperated voice,
the one she generally used for her colleagues.

Jay was shattered. Work was mayhem at this time of

year. He'd worked twenty-eight days without a day off and now the working day had extended from eight to ten hours, to fourteen to sixteen. It wasn't just that. Christmas was supposed to be 12 days wasn't it? Some people, Nicola included, seemed to want to make it last for almost two flipping months.

"I need sleep" he said truthfully, he'd been up since 3am and now it was almost 6pm. The farm shop was open until 8pm and Nicola was still keen that they pick a tree together.

Jay knew from last year that it didn't matter which one he said, Nicola would have already decided anyway. The hassle getting the dammed thing into their last place had been sufficiently memorable that he didn't want to go through that again.

The door banged loudly as Nicola made her way out.

An hour later he was woken by a persistent buzzing on the intercom. Nicola was downstairs in the garage.

"Can you come down? I need your help. I'm sorry about earlier." Nicola knew that she'd won. It was probably better that he hadn't been there anyway. She'd bought the biggest tree they had. Unfortunately, she'd neglected to consider that their nine-foot-high ceiling couldn't accommodate a seventeen-foot-tall tree.

Jay spent the next two hours ringing various friends to see if anyone had a suitable saw. Nobody did. The tree spent the night in the garage. Nicola gloated quietly to herself back in the flat.

After work the next day, Jay made the long drive to the garden centre where he bought what had to have been the most expensive bow saw in creation.

It took him an hour to trim the tree down, and another hour and a half to load all the trimmings into his car and take the wretched stuff to the dump. He was covered in sap and scratched. The trimmings had bled sap all over the car. The scratches itched like crazy.

He did it all with good grace though. Nicola wanted a tree and he wanted Nicola to be happy, he'd just been exceptionally tired the previous day.

He thought he'd surprise her, so he spent the rest of the afternoon moving all the furniture in the lounge in order to fit the tree in. Next he clambered up into the loft and dragged down the box of decorations Nicolas mum had given them when she'd replaced all her own. The rest of the afternoon was spent decorating the tree and fixing the lights. It took hours.

Just after six, Nicola arrived home from work. Jay waited expectantly. She came into the lounge, took one look at the tree, and said "Why did you move the telly and sofa? I was going to put it in the window."

Jay set about rearranging the furniture while Nicola decided that as it was her night to cook, they'd have a takeaway curry.

At 7pm Jay received a text. "Bumped into Cindy, having a quick drink, back soon."

At a little after 9pm, Nicola reappeared with a bag of congealing Madras. She was giggly and euphoric from the vodka she'd been drinking. As Jay decanted curry into the microwave, she called through from the lounge "I love you, I really, really love you. Do you know what? Now you've changed the room, I think I preferred it the way you had it earlier."

"Oh forfuckssake" he swore quietly. "I'll sort it when I get back tomorrow." He'd had to undress the tree and fanny around with extra extension cables. Now she wanted the bloody thing back in the corner. "I really, really love you" She oozed across the kitchen to him. Jay could have used a drink himself at that point, but as he had to drive at 3am again, he didn't dare take a chance.

"I love you too" he answered doing his best to remember some of their better moments.

"I saw Roger and Gwen when I was out, they said they'd pop by tomorrow. It would be nice if it could be sorted by then. Will you be back in time? "

Roger and Gwen were the couple they rented the flat from. Jay knew that tomorrow was going to be one of the busiest yet, and he might not get back until four.

"What time are they coming?" he hoped it wasn't going to be a long visit, they were nice enough people, but he was exhausted.

"Oh I'm finishing early tomorrow, so I said six o'clock."

Jay felt his heart sink.

The next day, Jay arrived home back at home just before four thirty. Nicola was already there and had put on her Maria Cary Christmas CD, and was working her way down a bottle of Baileys. There was no time to take a shower. Jay moved furniture while Nicola supervised. It was a Herculean effort, but he managed it. He paused to tidy up the tree once it was sitting back in the corner where he'd had it the afternoon before.

"I've got a surprise" Nicola announced and disappeared into the bedroom. She came back with an enormous box which had evidently been delivered that afternoon.

"I got us some new decs." She smiled "Those others are all looking a bit tired."

"I really need a shower." Jay was fit to drop now and only just clinging on by his fingernails.

Okay honey, I'll make a start. What's for dinner? It's your turn tonight." Nicola reminded him.

Jay made his way to the bathroom.

He was mid-shower when the doorbell rang. While

Nicola ushered Roger and Gwen in, he hurriedly finished showering and tugged clean clothes over his poorly towelled body.

Nicola had invited their landlords into the kitchen where she'd somehow magicked up a saucepan of mulled wine. It smelt lovely. They exchanged pleasantries and Gwen produced a Christmas card from her handbag.

"Would you like to see our tree?" Nicola asked.

There was Hmm-ing

Nicola went first with Jay behind her. Roger and Gwen followed. Jay had to admit, the tree looked spectacular.

Wow! He said impressed and then quietly to Nicola "How much did that lot cost?"

She took his hand and gave it a squeeze. "It was a bargain. I got the whole lot for £300." She paused to see his reaction and then added "I hope you don't mind; I raided your tip jar."

Jays tip jar had held £240, all hard earned, and he'd been planning to put it towards the new washing machine they desperately needed.

He didn't have time to react.

"Oh" said Gwen.

"Oh" said Roger.

There was an uncomfortable silence for a few seconds and then Gwen said, "Well this is awkward".

Jay and Nicola didn't understand. Roger took it upon himself to remind them.

"I'm really sorry but it says in the contract, artificial Christmas trees only please. It's a fire risk and the last tenant ruined the carpets."

"It is in the contract. Oh Nicky love, I'm really sorry, but we did make it clear." Gwen added helpfully, and then "Roger bought a new shredder a couple of weeks ago didn't you love? If you can't give it to someone, we'd be happy to help dispose of it."

Jay went into the kitchen and poured himself a very large glass of mulled wine.

5. SHOPPING

Helena had a list, and she was proud of it. In previous years she'd had to order gifts for her family from catalogues, because she didn't usually have a minute to spare herself in December, and she loathed trudging around the shops anyway.

Everyone wanted her professional services in December it seemed. Marriage Guidance and reconciliation, relationship counselling and therapy for trauma were in high demand as everyone prepared for the annual ordeal. January would be busy too.

In order to avoid all the family politics of her own, Helena always volunteered to help with the soup run for the homeless on Christmas day, just as she did on evenings and weekends for the rest of the year.

Helena was acutely aware of the flow of gifts between the super privileged and the contrast with the people she was trying to help give a lift back into housing and society.

Helping on the soup run had given her a valid reason to turn her phone off, and now after ten years of following the same routine, her family had finally stopped trying to pressurise her into taking part in the whole ghastly business. David, bless him, her partner, completely understood. He generally worked Christmas day too. The police control room always received notifications of all sorts of domestic incidents. David volunteered for the duty that day for several reasons, one of which was to spare his colleagues.

Helena looked at her list. It wasn't that she was mean or unkind, in fact she bought gifts for people and sent little things as thank you's all year round. She always remembered birthdays and she made special efforts for weddings and even just random tokens of appreciation. Helena's problem with Christmas, apart from the huge expense and the massive body of pressure to conform, was that she bitterly resented being told that on this mandatory day. On the 25th, people were expected to exchange gifts! The adverts and magazines told them so. Gifts which in most cases, the giver struggled to afford, and the recipient didn't need.

Helena had a strategy now though, if they expected bloody tat, masquerading as beneficial goodies, then that was what they'd get.

She would go to the retail park first, and then head into the vast temple for the exploitation of the weak minded, that was her local 'shopping centre'.

Halfords was pleasing. She bought Brian, her younger brother some car mats. They had an intense red and black tartan pattern. They'd be ideal. No one in the family had any connections to Scotland.

For her father she bought a motorised car polisher. Apparently it did the same thing as a soft cloth. As a last minute she added a pair of driving gloves. She didn't know if wearing them made anyone a better driver and in her lifetime cars had all been fitted with heaters. She supposed that if Dad ever wanted to go anywhere in his Volvo in the snow with the windows down and the heaters turned off, they might come in useful. As a last thought she bought him a box of toffees. They played havoc with his teeth, but he'd appreciate the thought.

She packed the big carrier bag into the boot of her Micra.

The shopping centre was a mass of enormous garish illuminated plastic hexagons that she suspected might have been intended to represent snowflakes. Alternatively, they could have been some sort of magical Illuminati symbol designed to hypnotise people into parting company with their cash. If they were, they were definitely working.

For her mum for the first part, she found a nice woollen hat, scarf, and glove trio in a fancy box. It was almost identical to the set her mum kept giving her every year. Mum liked black, even though it showed up the dog hairs. By Helena's reckoning mum must have at least seven similar hats now, but mother kept giving them to her too, and she wanted to make a point that she really didn't need any more, she only had one head. Next she went to Boots looking for one of those bubbling infra-red foot spars, the ones people used twice and then stashed under their beds until they tried desperately to offload it at a car boot sale three years later. Boots predictably had a huge stack of the things. She bought an extra bottle of lavender oil and some Radox to go with it.

She went back to the carpark to offload and then braced herself to head back in.

Norma, her sister-in-law, was a terrible cook and so in Debenhams there was an array of sets to help the incompetent.

Siegfried St John Barclay's 'Lets cook authentic Indian' came in a nice pack with a glossy book, six types of spices in neat little tins which were probably impossible to open without spilling the contents all down the front of the opener, and a four-section stainless steel bowl for serving brinjal pickle, Mango chutney and that yogurty cucumber stuff no one ever ate. Perfect! It was too big for the basket, so she tucked it under her arm.

There was also an 'Italian essentials set.' There was another glossy book and a clear caddy of brightly coloured pasta twists that was big enough to hold about a quarter of a bag of conventional pasta. It had a nice picture of the Colosseum on the lid. Helena giggled, oh the irony, to give that as a Christmas gift when her main memory of the Colosseum was that the Romans used to feed Christians to the lions there. The box also held a very special pizza cutter. This one had a genuine wooden handle the packing informed her. Wild eh?

Helena paused to consider how a tool such as a pizza cutter had become so commonplace. They must have been created in an area where for some reason, there were no sharp kitchen utensils and the locals had gotten tired of trying to hack their pizzas into neat portions using a spoon.

That was her brother Bill sorted too then.

Lastly, for family anyway, was her sister Emma. Emma had struck lucky several years earlier when she and her husband had been decorating their little two bedroomed house in Salford in Manchester. Jonathon had been in the loft fitting some insulation when he'd come across a box of paintings and charcoal drawings of stick figures, all set in the streets in the local area.

Most were unsigned, but five out of the 22 had the name L.S.Lowry in pencil at the bottom.

The subsequent auction had left Emma and Jonathon several million pounds richer.

Emma unfortunately, had no sense of taste. Jonathan, or Lettuce as he was more usually referred to in his absence, just went along and did as he was told. They'd bought a big ten-bedroom Georgian Rectory in Harrogate and had immediately began tearing out the inside and rearranging it. What they'd done in the garden was unforgivable. Four mature laburnums and around twenty lilac and fruit trees had been felled to make way for a swimming pool and a lawn which was now covered in concrete copies of Romano-Greek sculpture, plus a few gnomes.

Emma was impossible to buy for. She already had everything. Then again, the rest of Helena's family also had far more than they could ever use. Christmas was Christmas though and they were all addicted to the rituals.

It didn't help that Helena and Emma didn't see eye to eye on very much. Emma liked her collection of pet hamsters, she hated cats, and she always voted Tory. She loved spending money and made shopping a hobby. Her house was literally piled high with 'Stuff' she'd bought and never used. She loved to be seen at Ascot and Wimbledon and the Chelsea flower show, even though she had no interest whatsoever in horses, tennis, or flowers.

Helena loved cats, supported Greenpeace, and hated exploitation and waste. She liked to work quietly and avoided crowds. She like order and tidiness.

Helena had a couple of things on her list for Emma but sadly, she just couldn't find them. Emma didn't read books although she bought a lot to try to convey the impression that she might. Helena had thought about getting her Marie Kondo's book.

Emma loved Disney films, but all the titles Helena had hoped to find, had sold out too.

Frustrated now, and eager to get away from the constant tinkle- plunking-jingle of Christmas music, Helena made her way to Dingles hoping inspiration would strike.

She worked her way up through the four floors looking at clothes, kitchenware, cushions, linen, and picture frames. There was nothing here remotely suitable.

She was about to give up and made her way back downstairs. She decided to leave the shop on the opposite side from where she'd entered, perhaps she could find something in Waterstones.

She stepped off the escalator and there in the middle of all the china ornaments and figurines, was the perfect thing. She scooped up one in a box and took it to the till.

"Would you like this wrapped madame?" The pleasant young woman asked her.

"Oh, yeah, sure, great, thanks."

Helena made her way back to the car. David being the star he was, would do the wrapping and then she'd just drop everything off at mum and dads on Christmas eve, and then make a hasty retreat.

Everyone was sorted!

Helena was especially pleased with the figurine for Emma. In addition to Disney films, Emma loved The Hobbit.

The china limited addition figure of Sméagol with a fish was perfect!

Happy Christmas everyone!

6. CHRISTMAS JUMPERS AND SANTA OUTFITS

Dear readers, I am merely the narrator of these tales, and perhaps I should just stick to telling the stories. There are so many things about the season which leave me befuddled, and these things come high on my list.

Fancy buying a jumper that you only get to wear for a maximum of one week a year. On that basis, if the girls and boys in marketing can get it sorted, you'll need a few dozen more for all the different 'Special days'.

Just imagine the potential of Mother's day, Valentines, perhaps a nice picture of Jesus on the Cross for Easter Sunday? Relevant and a great talking point don't you think?

It's a polyester and nylon extravaganza! Nice one all you faithful recyclers.

I can't ever picture Betty Winsor coming out to make

her speech in one, but I can easily imagine Kate and Willy-boy pulling them on for a bit of 'We're getting down with the plebs' and dressing their poor unfortunate sprogs in them.

Modern times eh? Andy could have one too, perhaps it would help him attract a few more underage girls?

Santa outfits abound too of course. We have the annual Santa Christmas fun run in my hometown.

It all seems quite incongruent. For one thing, all the runners are skinny, it just looks wrong.

I always struggle with the term Fun-Run too. To me, that's an oxymoron if ever there was.

The thing I find more disturbing is the historical context.

Ho-Ho-Ho was what was said during medieval plays in order to tell the audience that the Devil was about to appear..."oh no not Satan".

Now then, what's that an anagram for?

Oh do come on, a fat bloke who sneaks into your house and slips silently into children's bedrooms, on route, quaffing literally thousands of glasses of sherry? And then he gets back on his sleigh. It's like a promotion campaign to say all of us lot shouldn't drink-drive, but if you're Santa, hell now, just go for it!

It's just wrong isn't it?

As for flying reindeer, as Nanny Ogg would say, oh deary, deary me.

In Sami culture, the true shaman feed fly agarics to the herd and then drink the urine in order to experience the hallucinogenic effects without the toxins that would otherwise make them chunder.

Perhaps that's where the idea comes from that reindeer fly?

Incidentally, I know a great spot where fly agarics grow on Dartmoor, so if anyone wants to test the theory, let me know and we'll sort something out for you.

Going back to Santa, people seem to believe the myth that the red and white figure we know today was invented by someone at the Coca-Cola company.

On that basis, by wearing the outfit, you'd be helping to promote type 2 diabetes then.

Given the amount of sugar we'll all consume over the next few days, how appropriate. (That reminds me, I'd better get some Pepsi to put in my rum)

There's a figure who takes part in Masonic initiations who has an outfit exactly like the red and white Santa character. I wonder what that's all about?

I see that Satan outfits online go for £10 up to £200, nice little earner for someone that.

If you dip into folklore, you'll discover that Elves aren't particularly pleasant creatures either.

The biggest waste of money and resources, and the greatest contribution to pointless environmental destruction though, has to go to the Christmas cracker paper hat.

Sheesh, honestly. I'm bewildered that people still actually buy those bloody things. I don't think anyone ever kept one on for more than half an hour.

Why? Just why?

You can call me a Humbug, and you'd be right.

However, there's an awful lot going on here that no one ever questions, and that I really don't understand.

I don't want to begrudge anyone of their enjoyment, but quite honestly, the whole ghastly business leave me baffled.

7. THE CHRISTMAS PARTY

Some people look forward to them, some people avoid them like the plague. Rachael rather enjoyed them. Perhaps it was the big sigh of relief knowing that everything there was to do, had been done.

Working in a Royal Mail delivery office was intense at any time, but the six weeks leading to Christmas would have tested Hercules himself.

The mail volumes built and built so that everyone started an hour then two then three earlier. At the other end of the day, the hours extended too.

Most of the mornings were good humoured, although repeatedly hearing Cliff, Shakey and Noddy on the radio became excruciating by about the 2nd of December. Kind souls would bring boxes of biscuits and mince pies to the office to show their appreciation. The posties would load up on sugar and sausage rolls before setting out to battle the elements and deliver their heavy loads.

One of the really lovely things was when appreciative recipients came to the door with a card or a bottle of something. Fivers were pressed into delighted hands with the words "Here, have a drink on us".

The effect on moral was wonderful.

In every office though, as the volumes increased, someone would always crack under pressure and have a very public drama. In Rachael's delivery office, the first to crack was usually Andrew in the office. Andrew had to count extra Special Deliveries and scan them in as received and then allocated. It was all too much for him. Andrew avoided going out on any delivery and had perfected the art of looking busy many years before when he'd got his feet under a desk. He was the only person in the history of Royal Mail to be issued company slippers. Ironic really that of all of the team, he was the one who worked the least hard, but managed to bleat and grumble the loudest. Eventually this would escalate to a full scale melt down with shouting and door banging as a few parcels were roughly scanned.

No one could have a drama quite like Andrew.

In the new year he would have to go sick for two weeks, knowing that for the posties, January was just as intense as December. He'd make sure he started coughing and doing his 'I feel poorly' routine about a week before Christmas. Rachael found him really rather tedious. That didn't stop her being nice to him though, some of the time.

Rachael was the union representative and she often had to 'advise' Andrew to moderate his behaviour towards his colleagues.

It was a shame really. There were times when he could be funny and helpful, gracious, and genuinely charming.

Rachael had arranged this year's get together. No one could agree on what to do, and there were different ideas from the twenty-eight posties regarding Indian meals, Bowling, Chinese, Karaoke in one of the towns pubs, and the suggestion of a night of yoga, meditation and vegan nibbles from Matthew and Jessica. The last suggestion had gone down like the proverbial lead balloon.

All of those had been abandoned for one reason or another and everyone had finally decided that they would simply go to the social club. They would have a table in their own special area with some food and have a good old fashioned traditional piss-up.

It was scheduled for after work, Christmas Eve, 3pm.

The vast piles of cards and parcels were packed into pouches and drop bags, and leaving Andrew to sob in the office, the posties made their way out onto the streets for the last leg of a very long haul.

Later, they dribbled back into the office, exhausted, but satisfied that they'd done their best, and everything had been delivered to its intended destination. The newspapers printed rubbish every year about vast piles of undelivered gifts and cards. It simply wasn't true. If something arrived after the 25th, it was because it hadn't been posted and part of the job was absorbing flack.

It was a huge relief to everyone when the office was completely cleared, and the door was finally locked for a couple of days.

Rachael rushed home, dived in the shower, and then pulled on the clothes she'd set out the night before. Chris and Ray were already at the bar when she arrived just before three. The rest of her colleagues gradually trickled in.

It was strange seeing everyone dressed in their own clothes, you got used to seeing everyone in uniform all the time. "Wow! Rachael, you look fantastic!" Chris greeted her and leaned forward to give her a peck on the cheek. "Look at you. I never realised your alter-ego was a babe" was Rays offering.

"You two have scrubbed up quite well yourselves, I'm not used to seeing you both in long trousers. Very grown up." She laughed and then added "G & T please".

"It's a great turn out." Rachael said after taking her first sip.

"Yeah, and even better without Andrew" Ray put in.

"I don't expect we shall see Mr Dramatastic" Rachael answered using her pet name for Andrew. They generally fought like cat and dog over anything that required a decision.

It wasn't long before a few more arrived. All three Williams had brought their wives. Tom had brought his latest girlfriend, Lucy arrived with her girlfriend too, and to everyone's surprise, Tony turned up with Andrews wife Glenda. They were clearly on intimate terms.

One or two discrete questions were asked, and Glenda explained that she and Andrew had been living separate lives for ages. Tony lived just a few doors down and things had blossomed.

The music played, sausage rolls and cheese footballs were gobbled, and the drink flowed liberally, loosening tongues.

Several people, including Rachael, revealed exactly what they thought of Andrew.

More alcohol was consumed, and the posties became even louder and more boisterous. It was as if they'd just been let off life sentences, the atmosphere was positively hysterical.

It was all going wonderfully when a voice said, "Can I get anyone a drink?"

To the amazement of all present, it was Andrew. Andrew had never come to the Christmas piss-up before, not ever. Here he was though, and he seemed to have softened, as if the person they knew in the office was someone different entirely.

He'd shaved for one thing, and his customary stubble had given way to a firm chin and rosy cheeks. His hair wasn't just combed, it was fashionably styled and gelled.

His clothes were immaculate.

The voices were slow to respond and then Peter said "Yeah, okay mate, that's jolly decent of you, I'll have a pint with you, it's cider mate cheers."

"Anyone else?"

Andrew headed to the bar with a list of thirteen drinks.

"Well, what do we all think of that?" asked Susan.

"Well, I don't mind taking a drink off him, but he's still a twat." Tom injected with a laugh.

Glenda and Tony got up to leave.

"Got to go, got to get an early night." Tony winked and patted Glenda on her bottom. By the time Andrew returned, they'd gone.

The party got going again. There was more music, more food and then to everyone else's immense enjoyment, Sue managed to get Dave up on the dance floor.

"She's going for the kill" Peter laughed seeing that Sue was clearly steering her victim this year towards the mistletoe.

"You wouldn't get me under there Rachael asserted "Not for anything, or anyone. If Brad Pitt himself was under there, there's no bloody way I'd do that."

A few minutes later when Dave and Sue appeared to be eating one another under said mistletoe, their sympathetic colleagues applauded and cheered loudly.

The band came on. It has to be said, they rocked. The posties began to circulate around the club talking to old friends and accepting drinks from the people they'd served all year.

The band ended and it was time for the first few taxis to take the annihilated posties home. It only takes a small amount of alcohol on top of that much fatigue to ruin anyone, and the posties had drunk like fish.

"Goodnight mate," Chris called to Tom.

"I wanted to say goodnight to Rachael, have you seen her?"

Tom smirked and jerked a thumb toward a dark corner. Two people were busy snogging as if their lives depended on it.

"Oh my god...is that..."

"Yep" Tom answered brightly.

"Oh my word. Has anyone taken some photos?"

"Lucy is on it mate, hahahaha, and it's video."

The two looked on as Rachael and Andrew continued with their furious snogging.

They'd never be allowed to forget.

"I bloody love Christmas parties, there's always something special to remember." Tom announced.

"Me too"

Jeremy Moorhouse

8 MIDNIGHT MASS.

It was the night every vicar dreaded. All year round they would navigate their parishes and introduce themselves to those they didn't usually see in church. It was hard to fill pews these days as people's faith diminished and the formerly faithful turned to their new gods, their I-phones, and their televisions.

Tonight would be different though, and Martin knew that his little flock would be joined in the village church by a whole load of people who wouldn't usually set foot inside unless there was a funeral, a christening, or a wedding. Whatever it was, it was only because the aftermath involved alcohol. Tonight was worse, tonight most of the additional village idiots would have started drinking long before the service began.

Martin had begun drinking too. He usually carried a hip
flask and tonight he'd filled it with vodka hoping no one
would be able to smell it. He'd also downed a couple of
large ones before leaving the vicarage. The hip flask was
empty now, but he felt fine, and the vodka was helping
his tolerance levels hugely.

It was supposed to be a celebration. Martin thought
about his sermon "Unto us a son is born..." he hoped
that moron Barry wasn't going to be there. Barry was a
proud atheist and had brought a placard last year which
read 'I'm just here for the singsong and the free mince
pies.' Barry, although not a great asset to the
congregation, was at least honest. The placard was a bit
much though.

Martin was a man of faith who'd had a calling. He'd
been a lorry driver before becoming a man of the cloth,
and he'd once had a go at stand-up comedy at Butlins in
Minehead. He'd spent most of his time on stage dealing
with abuse from the audience. Afterwards he'd spent
months learning lines other comedians used to put
down hecklers.

Martin watched them shuffling in. There was a group of
his regulars and then dotted around the church were
some of the less frequent visitors. The aroma was like a
brewery. Most of this lot had clearly been in the pub
and there was shouting from one side of the church to
the other and lots of drunken euphoric hugging going

on. The ambient noise level was higher than the jets which regularly flew over the spire.

Those who hadn't been in the pub had probably had a few sherry's or Malibu's or whatever it was people drank these days. They teetered and lurched around the pews and font wondering where to sit. "Here mate, what time are you bringing out the sausage rolls this year?" a man dressed in an Arsenal football shirt shouted looking at Martin and waving his arms to make sure he caught the vicars attention.

It began. Martin attempted to welcome the faithful on this most special of nights. The back four rows were so loud he could barely be heard. Martin had to ask for quiet again and generally the noise level diminished with the exception of a young woman who, unaware that the entire congregation could hear her now, was telling her friend "...under the mistletoe and I fink they're out there shagging by the big Yew tree now" Martin, like the professional he'd always wanted to be, announced the first carol.

About half the congregation sang the correct words while those in the back sang the school versions "One in a taxi, two in a car" came floating across the beery smog.

By the end of the carol, most of the audience had settled down except for one particularly vocal little girl who kept demanding to know when Santa was coming and if he'd been to her house yet. She then informed the world in general that she wanted to go home. Her embarrassed parent's tried to hush the little darling, who then began to scream. Some of the more thoroughly lubricated at the back began laughing. Martin hurried on with the service. As he stood at the lectern, the vodka hit him in a wave, and he felt the church spin around him. He kept it together though and he began reading. Thank goodness he'd been rehearsing.

He stumbled a little, he might have been slurring, but so far as he knew, he'd gotten away with it.

"And now for our second song, hymn number 282, While shepherds wash their socks...erm watch their flocks, erm so sorry." Thankfully the music began. Less thankfully, the congregation joined in to crucify a second classic.

"....all watching BBC,
The Angel of the lord came down
And turned to ITV"

It was time for the sermon. Martin clung on to the rail as he ascended the pulpit. Three hundred pairs of eyes bored into him and for a moment he felt the chilling embrace of stage fright. He normally only spoke to twenty or thirty people at a time at most.

He took a deep breath and scanned the crowd. There right in front of him and underneath the pulpit was Barry. He was wearing a hoodie with the legend "It's all a load of bollocks" printed on the front.

Martin began "Unto us a son is born..."
"I'm not having any more kids." Barry answered back.

"And our father looks down on us from above"

"I'd like to know what his name is" Barry filled in "My
mum said she never knew what it was."
A few people laughed. Martin was losing his composure
but decided to forge ahead.
"On this special day when joy comes to the world" He
was feeding Barry material now.
"I'd like to 'ave a special day with Joy myself...Joy from
the Blacksmiths Arms though, not post-office Joy"
There was more laughter, and it was becoming louder.

Martin had had enough.

"Doesn't beer make a lot of noise when it's sloshing
around an empty head" he snapped back.

Barry was momentarily lost for words and so Martin
seized the advantage.
"It's good to know that there's at least one village
where the idiot hasn't gone to London"

Some of the crowd were a little perturbed by this, most
were enjoying the show immensely. They'd come for
carols, but this was far more entertaining.
"Oh you think you're funny now?"
Barry wasn't happy that the vicar was standing up to

him. He'd intended to harass the poor man until the end. Barry thought he was clever and funny when he was in fact neither.

Taking a line from Arthur Smith, Martin snapped back "Look, it's all right to donate your brain to science but shouldn't you have waited till you died?"

By now a few of Barrys neighbours had decided that they'd better not let things go any further, and they grouped around him and then ushered him down the aisle and out of the heavy oak doors.

Martin brushed himself down and felt himself flushing bright red as the vodka got a really good grip.

He decided to abandon the sermon and announced the next Carol. Everyone loved Silent night. From outside Barry could be heard shouting "You can't ban me.."

Martin was feeling wobbly now. He clung to the lectern and completely omitted the final section of the service. "Shall we have another Shong then? How about O little town of Bethlemmm? Everyone likes that one. Joyce, Joyce? What number is it?" The congregation approved. Joyce had been scheduled to play Hark the Herald Angels and so there was a frantic flicking though pages during an otherwise uncomfortable silence.

"187" She called back trying to retain some semblance of dignity.

Voices raised and the story was told in song one more time.

Martin really wasn't himself now.

"Well thanks everyone, thanks for coming, and have a very Merry Christmas"
He was rather surprised when the gathered inebriates began applauding.
"Are we having mince pies now then" A voice popped up from the back above the clapping.

9 THE BIG DAY!

Up early, really flipping early. It was supposed to be a day off wasn't it?

Hahahaha, fate laughed herself silly at that thought.

5am, the Turkey had to go in….panic…"I did defrost it properly didn't I?"

Next doors kids are obviously up, I can hear them shouting and jumping up and down on their beds.

Better feed the dogs and get them out for their walk. Oh yuk, look at the bloody rain! For once, just once couldn't it snow on Christmas day? (And then Uncle Bob and tedious Vera would get stuck at home and we wouldn't have to humour them, quiet snigger, tee-hee-

hee)

Oh, just look at the state of the tree. The cats have obviously had a wonderful time. What on earth is that all over the carpet? I can't believe it; Herman has actually found and opened the flipping catnip. No wonder he looks like he's off his box. Oh bless his whiskers.

Hmmm, best take the old man a cup of tea. Eueww, you can smell the beer from down here. Still Tom had a good time with his mates in the boozer, and he was hilarious when he stumbled in, well, until he started snoring anyway. I hope he wasn't drinking Newcastle. I'm sending him out to the shed if he starts making brown clouds again.

Right then, I'd better get busy with this lot. Richard said him and Tina have to go to her mums so it's just eleven for dinner, Hmm, I hope I've got enough sprouts.

Oh damn-damn-damn I forgot to pick up the ruddy Cranberry sauce. How could I possibly have forgotten?

Oo, movement from the boys room. They did well, it's almost 6.30, then again, they were still awake at 2am. It's so lovely to have our Rita here. It's so good to get the family all together. I do hope she doesn't have another flaming row with Richard like they did last year, and the year before, and the one before that...

I'm not having our Sue and Chris monopolising the telly

again either. I want to watch the Sound of Music not some Disney torture session.

The clock moves forward.

Phew I could do with going back to bed. "Could one of you come and help dry up please?" Oh look at all that wrapping paper, what a shame. Oh my, what are we going to put all this plastic and cardboard in? The recycling bins already full. Still, it looked lovely there all piled up under the tree. Perhaps I can give that foot spa to our Rita. She might use it. I did tell Tom I didn't need anything. Bless him, at least the paper shredder will be useful.

I'd better take a dishcloth with me when I go back in the lounge, there's chocolate handprints everywhere. I hope they're going to eat their dinners. They haven't stopped eating chocolate since they got up.

Right, where was I, oh yes, paracetamol for Tom. Glass of snowball for me I think. I could get used to this daytime drinking.

"Can someone answer the phone please? ....I SAID CAN SOMEONE ANSWER THE TELEPHONE PLEASE?"

Ding-dong

Oh hello Uncle Bob, hello Vera, it's really lovely you could make it.

Oh no thanks Vera, I'm doing just fine in the kitchen

thanks. Why don't you go through to the lounge? (...and bloody well stay there...)

I hate peeling sprouts. Nearly sliced my thumb off dong the turnip too, surly someone can invent an easier to peel turnip?

Right then, what's next? Oh yes, fifteen pounds of spuds.

'Ding-dong'

"CAN SOMEBODY GET THAT."

"I SAID CAN SOMEBODY GET THAT!"

"THERE'S SOMEBODY AT THE DOOR!"

Oh flipping heck, I'll get it myself. As if I didn't have enough to do already.

"Oh hello Trevor, happy Christmas Mary. Hello Bridgette, you look lovely. Oh Bill, thank you, you're so thoughtful, I'd better find a vase for them. (Flowers? Where the hell am I going to put a vase of flowers? Oh flippin heck)

Yes come through, who wants a drink?

Tom, Tom, TOM! Where's he gone now. Oh hell, I'm supposed to be doing the veg not being waitress.

Oh Bridgette, you're an angel, yes please love, there's a

big bag of carrots on the side in the utility room. Yes please love, all of them.

Oh that blimmin phone again.

Where on earth has Tom gone?

Phew I'm shattered already and it's only quarter to eleven.

Think I'll have another snowball.

I'd better go and phone our Bessie in a minute too. I wonder where mum and dad are? They should have been here by now.

"Yes love, the tea's in the china pot there. Do you mind making it yourself? I've got to do the bread sauce".

Oh dear, Kylies off again, I know she's only five, but does she have to scream like that? Phew, I'll be glad when they've all gone home.

Thank goodness.

Oh turn the radio up, it's my favourite, 'lalalalalalalala,' This is much better than that Lady in red that he did. That was just embarrassing.

"COMING LOVE. BEER? ALREADY? AH OKAY THEN"

Where on earth did I put down that corkscrew?

Another load, that's the forth lot of washing up this

morning. I wish those flipping kids would help, or Trevor, or Mary.

"Oh no thanks Mary love it's fine. Anyway, there just isn't enough room for us all in here. It's a kind thought though. Yes love, there's some ice in the freezer and there's more tonic under the stairs".

What time is it? Oh, almost twelve already. I think I'll have another snowball.

Only twelve hours left to go. Perhaps I can have a nap after dinner?

"HANG ON LOVE, I'LL BE IN IN A MINUTE, I JUST HAVE TO GET THIS GRAVY GOING"

Right then, what's next?

Oh yes, custard for eleven.

10 THE AFTERMATH.

Marion had woken with a metallic taste in her mouth and something which had felt like a light sabre had pierced her skull.

The night before was a blur.

She'd spent all day in the kitchen and had finally sat down just in time for Mary Poppins, whereupon she had

consumed…Oh my god she realised with horror, a
whole bottle of Baileys. That hadn't been the cause of
her current woes though, afterwards, and enthusiastic
to really get into the spirit of things when they'd played
charades and Cards against Humanity, she'd started on
the Cherry Brandy. How much had she drunk for
goodness sake?

Clifford was still asleep and snored quietly beside her.
He'd had the good sense to go to bed at around 10.30.
Marion had stayed up with her sister and niece until
almost 2am. What on earth was she thinking?

She decided she'd better eat something and get some
ginger inside her before her stomach caught up with her
head.

She wall walked down the stairs and let Barney out into
the garden for a wee, hoping the cheerful Cocker
spaniel wouldn't decide now was a good time to go
through the fence and wake up his friend Flossie next
door.

What time was it anyway? It was still dark outside.
Hmm, the blurry hands of the kitchen clock seemed to
indicate it was twenty to eight.

Marion rummaged in the drawer for the strong co-
codamol she'd been prescribed and then saved for
'special occasions'.

She felt her way around the kitchen and managed to feed Barney and make a pot of tea before slumping into a chair with a mug.

The stirrings in the Kitchen had alerted Anita, and Marions sister now joined her in the gently beating heart of the house.

"Morning" Anita offered brightly, and then observing her struggling sister "Oh dear" and she laughed before continuing "Oh Sis, you do suffer afterwards don't you?" She patted Marion affectionately on the arm as she went past."

"I made tea" Marion pointed feebly at the steaming pot "But I know you prefer coffee." Anita was already refilling the kettle.

She made a bit of a fuss of Barney and assembled the desired brew. She joined her sister at the table.

As she sat she said, "I'll do all the catering today, you wouldn't let me do a thing yesterday."

"Thanks Neet" Marion reached slowly for her mug and then remembered what was scheduled. "Oh god, what time are Mum and Dad coming?"

"You told everyone eleven sharp, lunch at noon." Anita reminded her and then added "You do remember you texted Auntie Doreen and Uncle Denis last night to invite them too don't you?"

"I did? Oh bloody hell. Why did you let me do that?"

Anita laughed again. "You know there's no stopping you when you get going. And Andrew and Lorraine."

"Oh god" Marion groaned.

"Do you think you'll still be okay to walk up Dragon Hill?" Anita took another mouthful of coffee.

"What? Oh god no…did I really suggest that? Oh god" Marion laid down on the table now.

"Yep" Anita answered brightly. "You said it would be a good opportunity to open a few windows, air the house, and let the smell of boiled swede and Brussel sprout farts out for a couple of hours."

"Nnnnnnnn" Marion groaned again.

"Marion?"

"Yes"

"Why don't you open your eyes?"

"Because I don't want to bleed to death."

Jeremy Moorhouse

11 THE THUMB TWIDLING GAP

Following the anti-climax of the 27th and 28th, everybody was fed of up with being confined. Outside it didn't begin to get properly light until after 9am and then it got dark again by 4.45. Everyone was fed up.

In James and Angela's house, everyone had retreated to their bedrooms now. It felt is if they'd all adopted pyjamas as daywear and only Angela had managed to dress herself completely since the 25th as she'd needed to venture out to the Spar shop for more milk.

James had made an essential trip too, but that was for cider, and he hadn't bothered to change out of his flannel joggers and slippers, despite Angelas disapproving look.

The days had been spent nibbling sweets and cheese,

interspersed with Turkey sandwiches. Once the boxing day aftermath was dealt with, the remainder of the time was consumed spending pointless hours scrolling through Facebook and Tick-tock while the new books they'd all been given sat gathering dust in their assorted new locations.

Rather than see this as a time to genuinely rest, recuperate and align with the season, they binged on alcohol, sugar, carbohydrates, social media, and television.

The realisation that work began again in just three days, sank in. By lunchtime, James and Angela were deep in discussion about their plans for New Year's Eve. The boys were still too young to pay much attention and would be happy in front of the television with James mum. Norma would probably work her way through half a bottle of sherry and then fall asleep in the chair. The boys would undoubtedly stay up watching television until Angela and James came back.

Chloe at nineteen, would be heading out somewhere with her friends, and would probably spend three remorseful days swearing she'd never drink again, just as she had done last New Year, and all through the festival season, and again on Boxing day. The best Angela and James could hope for was that their pretty daughter would dress in something marginally less revealing than a bikini and some leopard spot body paint this year.

This led them onto their current discussion. What should they wear? Most of the people in the village pub would be in fancy dress. It was part of the fun and spectacle...apparently. For James and Angela, it was the source of yet another expense, and another annual round of stress.

If they dressed up, they would inevitably come across someone who'd 'gone the extra mile' and hired proper theatrical gear and facial makeup, which just left them feeling cheap and inadequate.

If they just went out in their normal gear, it was as if they could feel everyone else's eyes scolding them.

The only time they'd really pulled it off was the year they'd gone out with a group of their friends dressed as Smurfs and had then had to repaint their hall and kitchen because they'd managed to smear blue body paint everywhere.

They decided to pop into town and look around the charity shops. Since Angela had been watching Marie Kondo, they didn't have any old gear to fall back on. She'd even persuaded her mum and dad to give up their treasures from the seventies and eighties. Angela regretted this now.

The charity shops were all open and were the busiest

places in town apart from the big pub with the open fire. They were too late. All the best stuff had already gone, and so unless they chose to go out as fashion victims from two years ago, their choices were severely restricted.

They returned to the car , dejected.

On the way back out of town, they were just approaching the local DIY store when Angela abruptly braked, and then turned sharply into the car park.

"I've got an idea." She said brightly.

It was surprisingly busy inside. They made their way to the decorating section where they picked up two sets of blue disposable paper overalls. Perfect!

The following evening, they set off for the pub. The outfits looked great. They'd had no trouble at all getting hold of blue surgical masks, blue rubber gloves and of course, the mandatory face shields.

Angela had borrowed the boys felt tips and drawn radiation hazard symbols on the fronts and written Biohazard in big black letters with a yellow and black flashed surround across the backs. Once the hoods were up, the effect was pleasingly realistic they both thought. They finished the outfits with wellington boots.

They didn't see anyone at all in the ten-minute walk to the Seven Stars, but there was a reassuring babble coming from inside as James reached for the door.

"Ready?" He asked.

"I think we've cracked it this year." Angela smiled back underneath her mask.

James yanked the door open.

There was a momentary lull in conversation as around forty-five people all looked towards the door to inspect the newcomers.

Forty-five people including the bar staff, all dressed in blue paper overalls. Every single one of them was wearing a face shield and a pair of blue rubber gloves.

12 AFTERWARDS

Getting a live tree had been Debbie's Idea. Not putting it in their small garden had been Dave's idea. Dave had seen the size that the tree next door had grown in just twenty years since Lucy, his neighbour, had planted it. It was four feet tall then and had cost just £2.50 per foot.

The tree surgeon had charged £1200 to take it down, which was around £30 a foot.

The gargantuan trunk still lay like a behemoth overshadowing everything around it.

It had been Debbie's idea to take the tree out to Stanton woods and plant it amongst others of its kind. It was Debbie's idea that Dave could do this on his day off on the second Saturday of the year.

It had been Dave's idea, knowing just how difficult it

was to dig a hole in the woods, to go equipped with a mattock and an axe to chop through any big roots he inevitably encountered while digging the hole.

It was Dave's idea to go early, before any inquisitive walkers might question what he was doing and so it was barely light when he set off.

It was also Dave's idea to stop in the layby by the main road rather than drive an extra three hundred yards and pull into the car park.

It was PC Joseph Tamblyn's idea to apprehend Dave when as he'd driven the patrol car past the layby, he'd spotted Dave emerging from the trees, plastered in mud, and armed with the mattock and axe.

It had been raining heavily and Tamblyn hadn't wanted to get the back seat of the patrol car wet, and so he and Dave had stood in the rain waiting for back-up to arrive to go and confirm the authenticity of Dave's tree planting explanation.

Dave was a bit miffed.

Dave drove home in silence apart from the occasional snarl at the radio which was telling him that if he hadn't been so stupid to fall for all that new year's day sale bollocks, he could now get an additional 15% off at DFS today.

He squelched in through the back door and stripped off his filthy soaking gear in the kitchen. There was a note on the kitchen table.

"Just nipped down to Sue, back in half an hour. PS you've been gone ages, did you bump into a friend or something?"

Dave went upstairs and ran himself a bath.

Debbie still hadn't come back when he settled himself into the soothing embrace of the warm, bubbly water.

Thank god that was done, it was truly horrible out there, a howling wind and the rain was verging on apocalyptic.

At least he didn't have to go out again today.

And at least that was it now for another eleven months. Dave hated Christmas. New year's eve was okay, but he detested the whole ghastly business when it came to Christmas.

He hated those bloody awful nonstop Christmas records.

He hated all the forced jollity and false sincerity as people he'd never set eye's on before bade him 'Happy Christmas.' He might be the next Harold Shipman for all they knew, and they were wishing him a Happy Christmas? Why?

Then there was all that terrible fat and sugar-based fodder masquerading as food.

Dave had studied nutrition, and when it came to what people ate at Christmas, there wasn't very much which was actually nutritional. No flipping wonder there was a flu and cold epidemic every year in January and February.

He hated tinsel with a passion and as for flashing lights, what a waste of time, money, and resources. He'd slipped in the loft last weekend when he'd been putting all theirs away, and then he'd spent the rest of the weekend fixing the plaster on the landing.

That was all irritating, but what he hated most was the pure avariciousness and greed of the event.

Debbie and Dave both earned a reasonable living. They lived in one of the most affluent countries in the world and enjoyed luxuries that 85% of the global population could only ever dream of. The bath he was sitting in being one of them.

They had so much stuff, and most of it served no purpose whatsoever.

Tat.

Debbie's sister had given them a 'Home is where the heart is plaque. His mum had given them yet another china piggy bank to add to the eight that were already on the sideboard. Dave shook his head. Why? Just Why? What was the point of all this cluttering garbage?

On the back of the bathroom door hung the brand-new dressing gown Debbie had bought him, and the one his mum had bought for him last Christmas, and the one his sister had bought for him the year before that.

So much stuff.

When Dave was eight, all the other kids had been given things like Operation and Mousetrap, Scalextric and Action men. Dave's parents had given him a set of gardening tools, the implication being that at eight years old, they now expected him to look after their garden.

Now that he was older, he'd have been chuffed to bits with a new border fork, or even better, a manure fork for when he turned the compost. But no, it had all gone wrong.

Useless shit, that was what Dave mostly got...and he didn't want anything in the first place anyway. Dave knew he was perfectly capable of buying anything he wanted, whenever he needed it, and he didn't really need anything at all.

All this Christmas business meant, was that he and Debbie had more clobber to try and accommodate in their little house, and then they were pressurised into finding some form of reciprocation.

He bit his tongue though and did it all to keep Debbie happy.

At least that was it for another year. He'd even persuaded Debbie to start filling a box for the car boot sales when they began again at Easter.

He heard the door downstairs. It was Debbie. She called up the stairs. "You're home then?"

"I'm in the bath love, I'll be down in twenty minutes."

"Oh, brilliant. I've just been chatting with Sue; she's been round the sales and says there's loads of brilliant stuff up for grabs in town. I need you to drive so we can go shopping."

Silence

"Dave? Dave did you hear me?"

Jeremy Moorhouse

ABOUT THE AUTHOR

Jeremy Moorhouse lives in Cornwall where he writes
about all the bizarre things which catch his attention.
If you laughed at this, then just type Jeremy Moorhouse
into the Books listing section on Amazon, where you'll
find a few more titles that will definitely make you chuckle!
Facebook.
Storyteller, Jeremy Moorhouse

Printed in Great Britain
by Amazon

34412660R00046